About the Author

Eric England is a retired power station engineer. Since taking early retirement in 2006, he has worked on Sony music forums as a moderator. He also works voluntarily in a community shop. *Natalie* is his first book. It was inspired by helping a young Italian lady, who was being harassed on the forum, and his love for music.

Natalie

Eric England

Natalie

Olympia Publishers
London

www.olympiapublishers.com
OLYMPIA PAPERBACK EDITION

Copyright © Eric England 2023

The right of Eric England to be identified as author of
this work has been asserted in accordance with sections 77 and 78 of
the Copyright, Designs and Patents Act 1988.

All Rights Reserved

No reproduction, copy or transmission of this publication
may be made without written permission.
No paragraph of this publication may be reproduced,
copied or transmitted save with the written permission of the publisher,
or in accordance with the provisions
of the Copyright Act 1956 (as amended).

Any person who commits any unauthorised act in relation to
this publication may be liable to criminal
prosecution and civil claims for damage.

A CIP catalogue record for this title is
available from the British Library.

ISBN: 978-1-80439-186-0

This is a work of fiction.
Names, characters, places and incidents originate from the writer's
imagination. Any resemblance to actual persons, living or dead, is
purely coincidental.

First Published in 2023

Olympia Publishers
Tallis House
2 Tallis Street
London
EC4Y 0AB

Printed in Great Britain

Dedication

I dedicate this book to my wife, Janet, and my children, Julie and Neil.

Chapter 1

Here I am, thirty-five years old and dumped for the fourth time by a girl.

I have never been in love, and as soon as I start to develop feelings for a girl, she leaves me for someone else.

Am I going to be alone all my life?

Will I ever find the right girl, as time seems to be slipping by me?

I thought that I should quit my job, as I am always travelling away from home. The trouble is that I really like my job and it pays so well, but it is not bringing me happiness. I don't have any family, as my parents both died of cancer. My mother was last, passing away two years ago, and I was an only child.

I decided that I would have a word with my boss Steve. I had known Steve for many years. There was a vacancy in the office and I would ask Steve about it.

I was well over-qualified for the position, but it would be a drop in money. I felt that I needed more stability in my life.

I walked into Steve's office. I sat and told him what I wanted. Steve thought for a minute, and said that they were looking for someone to head up to their new Chelmsford office starting next week. There was already someone there, but they were struggling to cope. The position would be only for six months until the office was up to full speed.

This would actually mean a pay rise instead of a drop, so I said I would do it. There was already a house available, but would have share with my deputy manager for the time being.

Everything was all set up, and I headed up to Chelmsford Monday morning.

Chapter 2

I arrived at the Chelmsford branch, and Chloe, the receptionist, showed me up to the manager's office.

Chloe knocked on the door, went in, and said, "Morning, Miss James, Mr Alan Ford is here to see you."

Looking out of the window was a woman with long, dark, almost-black hair. You could see her body tense when Chloe said my name.

She turned and I recognised her instantly. Natalie James.

She had not changed one bit from when I met her at university. Stunningly beautiful with an amazing figure. She still looked as cold as ever. She had been nicknamed the Ice Queen and was very difficult to talk to.

I had never seen her with a boyfriend at uni. The one person I did not want to see now.

Natalie recovered quickly, and walked over and shook my hand. "Surprised to see you here, Alan."

"You too," I replied. It had been a long time.

How on earth am I going to be able to work with this woman? I had tried to have a conversation with her many times at Uni with either 'yes' or 'no' answers.

Everyone, including the girls, thought there was something wrong with her. The two good things about her were her looks and her intelligence.

I knew why there was a problem with the office, as Natalie lacked communication skills. How was I going to be able to communicate with Natalie? I felt like leaving and returning back to Tunbridge Wells.

Natalie was thinking, *why has he come here? I had an enormous crush on him at Uni and I could never speak to him. Act cool, Natalie, and be normal as you are with the rest of the staff.*

Natalie surprised me next with a smile. I had never seen her smile before. It made her look even more attractive. Maybe she was not an Ice Queen after all.

She said, "please, sit down, we need to talk."

We had our first ever real conversation. She explained what she had done to date, and how she saw the way forward. I was actually quite impressed. Although, I saw several alternative ways forward.

Natalie thought, *great. Listen to what he has to say.*

I explained my ideas to her, and she listened intently without interrupting. When I had finished, she said, "I can see why they sent you up here, you have a lot of great ideas." I nearly fell off my chair.

Natalie thought, *this guy is really good at his job as well.*

I said, "maybe you could give me a tour to meet the rest of the staff?"

She smiled again, and said, "Follow me. We can have coffee when we return and chat some more."

Natalie thought, *going well.*

The tour went quickly, but I noticed a very stern look from Colin in finance.

We sat and talked over coffee, and I thought, *this is not the same girl I knew from Uni.*

Natalie thought, *Colin is still being an idiot.*

What had changed? There was no ring on her finger, but maybe she had a boyfriend. I spent the rest of the day settling into the office. I was feeling relieved on how well the day had gone when I remembered that I would be sharing a house with Natalie. How well would that go?

How are we going to get on in the flat together? Natalie thought.

Chapter 3

Natalie walked into my office just as I was filling in my daily report, which I always did every day anyway. "Time to go home," she said, "and get you settled in."

The house was not a house, but a two-bedroom flat, which was OK with me. I let Natalie use the bathroom first while I unpacked. Natalie shouted, "I'm out," and I went in the bathroom for a much-needed shower and shave. Also, a change of clothes.

Good, Natalie thought, *I think I will offer Alan a takeaway.*

When I came out, Natalie had a lot of takeaway menus on the table, and said that she thought it would be good to eat in and get to know one another over a dinner and wine. I did not need asking twice.

She said, "what do you fancy to eat?"

When I replied with 'Italian', she beamed a big smile and said, "Italian is my favourite."

I can't believe he said Italian; it is my favourite, thought Natalie.

We sat talking all night and I found out that she was half Italian. Her mother was Italian – that explained the black hair and slightly tanned skin. She had also lost both her parents in a car crash five years ago, and was an only child.

This is much better than expected, thought Natalie.

We got up to do the minimal washing up. She then, surprisingly, gave me a peck on the cheek and said goodnight. Natalie was annoyed with herself – she could have kissed Alan properly.

All through the rest of the week, we devised an amazing Action Plan together, which we were going to implement next week. Natalie thought that we worked so well together. Every evening, we had a takeaway with a glass of wine and went to bed.

Friday afternoon, I drove back to my apartment near Tunbridge Wells for a peaceful, relaxing weekend. Natalie thought. *I do not want Alan to go back home.*

I laid in bed Friday night, and I could not get Natalie out of my mind. I knew that I was falling for her big time, but did she feel the same way? I was missing her lovely smile, the wonderful conversation. Everything about her. I was getting a pit in my stomach every time I thought about her.

Natalie thought. *I cannot wait to see Alan again Monday morning.*

Sunday afternoon, that creep Colin knocked on Natalie's door. He forced himself in and was in a rage. What was wrong with him? He was married.

Colin started punching Natalie.

She fell and banged her head on the table. Colin got scared when Natalie did not respond. He left, saying, "That will teach you, bitch."

The weekend went very slowly for Alan, and he was so happy when he packed his car up with more of his belongings so that he did not have to return home for a while. He drove back to Chelmsford.

Chapter 4

I arrived at the office at 8.45 and went straight to Natalie's office.

She was not there. OK, so I was early, but Natalie always arrived early. I went to my office and waited. Nine a.m. went and passed. I went and saw Chloe to see if she knew anything. She said Natalie always contacted work if she was only going to be a few minutes late. I asked Chloe to come with me to the flat, as I was getting worried.

Chloe thought, *OMG, what is happening?*

We arrived at the flat, and to my horror, Natalie was laying on the floor looking very battered. Chloe screamed. Chloe thought Natalie was dead. I calmed her down and told her to ring 999 for the police and an ambulance. I went straight to Natalie to feel for a pulse; it was OK, but shallow. Her breathing was shallow as well. I started to well up seeing her like this. How long had she been laying there? Why did I leave her alone?

She had been beaten badly. The whole flat had been ransacked, so was it just a robbery. Chloe thought. *Alan must really care for Natalie. what had been going on in this flat?*

The police arrived first and quickly took charge, questioning Chloe and I.

The ambulance arrived shortly afterwards, and they removed Natalie to the stretcher after the police had taken photos.

I so wanted to go with the ambulance, but the police still wanted to know if anything was taken. I could not answer for what was in Natalie's room. My room had hardly been touched, and nothing appeared to be missing.

I rang Steve to tell him what had happened. He said he would drive up later in the day to help out.

Steve was thinking, *what is happening? I had read both their files and they were made for each other. He knew they both went to the same University and were both still single.*

When he had been recruiting Natalie, she let slip there was a great guy at Uni, but never any serious relationships. This made him think of me, and wondered if it was. He had a hunch he was right. When I asked about the change of work, it gave him a chance to test his theory.

I took Chloe back the office and walked round the offices. In finance I asked where Colin was, and they said he had not turned up for work. I asked where he lived, and to give him a call. I suddenly remembered the look he gave Natalie and I when we went on the tour last Monday.

I left and went round to his house. His wife answered and said that she had not seen him since Sunday morning. She said he had been in a bad mood all week. She was pleased he went, as he sometimes got violent.

I decided to ring the police and tell them about Colin. They said that they would look into it. I rang Broomfield hospital to find out how Natalie was, but they would not say over the phone.

I went back to the office, and everyone was upset. It seemed like Natalie had made an impression on everyone. Seeing the way the office was working, I was wondering why Steve had sent me up here. Natalie was doing a great job.

I went to HR to see the results of the background security checks that were carried out on Colin before he was employed. They were missing from the file. No one had booked them out. They would have only been allowed to be booked out to me or

Natalie anyway.

I went to Natalie's office to check if they were there. Not there either.

Steve arrived at three p.m., and I filled him in on what had happened. I rang the police and they had finished with the flat. Steve stayed at the office, and I took Chloe with me to the flat. She was brilliant, and helped me clean the flat.

Chloe thought, *here is a really great guy*.

I took Chloe home, came back, and had a long shower. I was not hungry, so I decided to drive to the hospital to see if I could see Natalie.

She had been awake for a short time, but was asleep. When I said who I was, they let me in to see her. I so wanted to cuddle her and tell her how I was feeling. I sat until visiting was over. I rang Steve and we met for a drink and a chat.

We could not believe how Colin had slipped through our security check. Steve had been going through all of Colin's finance work and found a number of discrepancies. It was looking as if we may have to call the police.

Chapter 5

I called Steve Tuesday morning and said that I was going to the hospital first. When I arrived, the police were already there interviewing Natalie, so I had to wait.

When I eventually was allowed in, Natalie gave me such a lovely smile. I went over and gave her a gentle cuddle and peck on the forehead. She could see that I had a tear in my eye and asked me why. I just said it. "I am falling in love with you."

Natalie started to cry. She said that she had been waiting fifteen years to hear me say that. I could not believe it. She said that she had such a crush on me at Uni, but was too shy and just clammed up. I said that she was quiet with everyone. She sobbed and said that she was being stalked and scared all the time.

That explained a lot. I so wish I had asked her out at Uni, but we were both young.

Natalie turned to me and said, "Please kiss me gently." I did and I was in heaven. This must be what true love is about. She said that she was falling in love with me as well. Natalie could not believe that what she had longed for so long was really happening.

I asked her what happened at the flat. She said that Colin had been pestering her for a date for ages and she could not stand him. She found out that he had a criminal record for violence, and told him that he was going to be dismissed.

"He turned up at the flat Sunday afternoon and forced his way in and started hitting me. I must have passed out, because the next thing I remembered was waking up in here."

I kissed her again. Longer and more passionate this time. I said that I could not wait to have her back home at the flat. Home, I actually said home.

She said that she was not badly hurt with only a few bruises, but had a concussion so was being kept in for another day. I had to go to let Natalie rest, but promised to come back later.

Colin was on the run after what happened in the flat. He thought that he had killed Natalie. He booked a Motel room and laid on the bed thinking.

That bitch would not go out with me at Uni as much as I tried. I followed her everywhere and she still did not appreciate me. I lost touch with her when we left Uni, but could not believe my luck when she turned up at Crescent Employment Agency.

She did not recognise me as my hair was cut short instead of long and it was starting to grey prematurely.

Why did that Alan have to turn up? I am sure Natalie had a crush on him. He is going to take her away from me. He has to be taken out of the picture, if not it will have to be Natalie. If I can't have her no one will.

I went back to the office and Steve was there. Everyone was over the moon that Natalie was going to be OK.

Steve went back the next day, and I went and picked Natalie up from hospital. She wanted to go into work before she went home for more rest.

They were all so pleased to see her, and she had gentle cuddles from everyone. Was it me or was she really happy? I took her to the flat, kissed her, and made her go to bed. I said that I would bring Italian later. She flashed me one of her beautiful smiles.

Natalie was laying on the bed, thinking, I really do love Alan. I will put on my most revealing dress for him when he gets home.

I returned later and found that Natalie had put a very sexy dress. I just stood there and said, "WOW."

She came up to and gave me a very passionate kiss. Natalie pulled away and said, "I love you."

I looked at her, and for the first time ever, I said, "I love you."

Natalie found some candles and we had a romantic candlelit dinner. We put some romantic music on, and danced slowly around the room. She said that she was feeling tired, so I walked her into her room.

She said, "will you just lay with me tonight?" So, I laid with her all night cuddling her.

I woke up first the next morning and went into the shower. I heard a noise, and Natalie walked into the shower with me. The bruises were healing, and she looked absolutely stunning. We kissed and cuddled while we showered. We had to rush as we were late, so Natalie rang up work to say that we would be a few minutes late.

Everyone was so pleased to see Natalie back at work and wanted to talk to her. I went to my office and started catching up with work. There was an email from Steve addressed to both myself and Natalie.

When Natalie eventually came in the office, I pulled up a chair and we read it together.

Hi, you two lovers,

I knew you would work well together. The Action Plan you

both created is excellent and we will be using it in all our branches in future.

I have decided to keep you both working together, so you may both need to move around our branches to implement the action plan. Don't panic – it will not be for another six months.

Well done to you both.

Steve

PS. Make sure you invite me to the wedding.

Natalie blushed. I said, "What do you think?"

She replied, "Ask me tonight."

I said, "about the action plan?" I got a slap for that. I thought, *how did Steve know?*

I put my head into Natalie's office and said, "Lunch." I knew she must have been hungry, as we had skipped breakfast.

We popped into a cafe and had a quick coffee and sandwich. Then I grabbed her hand and said, "Come with me." I stopped outside a jeweller and said, "What ring would you like when I ask you?" She started to cry and gave me a big kiss and took me inside. She picked one immediately.

She shyly replied, "I was looking at that one last week. I was just hoping, as I had fallen in love with you."

The ring was perfect, and I bought it.

Chapter 6

The girl behind the counter screamed. I turned and saw Colin coming at us with a knife.

I pushed Natalie out of the way as he slashed the knife. I kicked the knife out of his hand and punched him hard. I had taken karate as a youngster, and still practiced. Colin fell to the ground, and I pinned his hands behind his back.

Just then, a plain-clothed policeman jumped in. Colin was handcuffed and taken away.

Natalie screamed, "Alan, you are hurt!" I had not noticed, but blood was dripping from my left arm.

The shop attendant rushed in with a First Aid kit and bandaged my arm. The cut was pretty deep, so Natalie drove me to the hospital.

We did not get away until six p.m., so we went back to the flat.

I said, "let's have a quick change and shower. I am taking you out to dinner tonight." Natalie rushed to the bathroom, showered, and went into her bedroom to change." I followed her in the shower when she was finished.

Natalie had dressed in this amazing red dress. OMG did that fit her body so well!

We went for an Italian meal at 'Alan's' and I ordered Champagne. When it arrived, I got down on one knee and said, "Natalie, I love you, will you be my wife?"

She jumped up and said, "YES, YES, YES!" Everyone

turned and looked and started applauding. I put the ring on Natalie's finger and kissed her.

The rest of the evening was blur. I know we did not stop talking all evening. I can't remember if the meal was good or bad.

We got back to the flat and just stood kissing for ages. Natalie then said, "take me to bed, but please be gentle with me as this will be my first time."

I could not believe that a girl as beautiful as Natalie had never had sex.

"Why have you never been with a man? You are thirty-five years old."

She replied that it was the first time she has wanted to give herself to anyone. I felt so privileged, picked her up and took her to her bedroom. Now, I had slept with four other women in the past, but what I had with Natalie was perfect and very special.

Natalie turned to me after and said, "I am so glad I waited for the right person. That was so special for me."

We kissed and cuddled over and over again until we fell asleep in each other's arms.

We went to work the next day and called everyone into a tightly-packed Conference room.

Natalie held out her hand, and said, "We are engaged." They all cheered and applauded and wanted to look at Natalie's ring. She looked so happy and radiant. I really could not wait to marry this girl.

Chloe came up to me said she knew from the start that we would be together. "I hope she asks me to be a bridesmaid, as we are the best of friends."

They all went back to their jobs, and Natalie and I were alone in the conference room. I said we should go back to what we get paid for.

I went into my office and phoned Steve. Told him about the engagement. He said he already knew. Texts were flying everywhere about us. We had become the talk of the whole company.

Friday morning, Natalie asked me if I was going back to Tunbridge Wells for the weekend. I said, "After last weekend, I am not leaving you on your own ever again."

She said, "I did not mean that, it is just that I would like to come with you to see where you lived."

I said that I was not planning to, and that I would love to, but let us make it the next weekend. She looked at me puzzled, and said, "I think you are up to something."

I said, "I am, but it is a surprise."

She smiled, gave me quick kiss, and said, "I am starting to read you like a book." Natalie went back to her office.

I picked up the phone to Chloe. "Have you said anything to Natalie? She suspects something is going on."

"Not said a word, but there is a lot of whispering going on in the offices."

Friday night, back at the flat, Natalie said, "What is going on? Everyone stops talking when I walk in the room."

I said, "It is a surprise. Would you like a Chinese takeaway tonight with wine and candles?"

She kissed me and said, "Yes please." I knew that I had only temporarily changed the subject. Natalie did not bring it up again, but we had another amazing night in bed.

In the morning, I said, "Would you like to go shopping?" What woman does not like shopping?

Natalie said yes immediately. I walked her past a lot of dress shops and said that they were beautiful dresses for a beautiful lady. She skipped up and down like kid and said, "Are you going to buy me a dress? No one since my mother has done that for me."

I took her inside, and she must have tried on ten different dresses. She narrowed it down to two, and asked me which one I liked. I said I liked both, and I bought both of them for her. She said, "I love you so much," and kissed me right there in the store in front of everyone.

We got back to the flat, and Natalie could not wait to try the dresses on again. I shouted out to her, "Which one are you wearing tonight when we go out?"

She crept back in the room and said, "Where are we going?" I said it was a secret. I could see she was busting to find out.

Natalie came out in the classy blue dress and asked if it would be OK for tonight. I said it was perfect. "You look absolutely amazing." Natalie changed back into her figure-hugging jeans and came and sat on my lap, put her arms around my neck, kissed me passionately and then said, "I love you so much and have never been this happy."

She sat there all afternoon and we talked about when we were going to get married. I said, "As soon as possible. What type of wedding do you want? Chloe has already hinted to me that she would love to be a bridesmaid."

Natalie said, "I know. She has been my best friend since I came here. She is such a lovely girl. I think that a quiet registry office wedding would be best for me."

I said, "OK, that will be quicker to organise as well." We seemed to agree on everything.

Chapter 7

Natalie went to town with her dressing up, and spent ages making herself up. She stepped out of the bedroom and said, "What do think?" I said she was beautiful enough for a prince. She gave me a peck on the lips and said, "I already have my prince."

"Right," I said, "let's go." I could see the excitement mounting in her. The taxi was waiting for us. He took us to the restaurant where I proposed. Natalie looked puzzled. I took her in, and everyone from work was there.

They shouted, "Surprise!"

The tables were laid out for a private party with a band playing softly in the corner. There was also a space cleared as a dance floor. I said, "You cannot have an engagement without a party." She hugged me and was crying with happiness. When she finally pried herself away, Chloe led her to the bathroom to tidy up her make up.

When they returned, Natalie was beaming. She skipped up to the band and said, "Play something romantic." She then came up to me and led me to the dance floor. We really did dance cheek-to-cheek with 'The Lady in Red'. It reminded me of our first romantic evening together when Natalie came out of the hospital. The evening was a total success, and Natalie even got a bit tipsy. When it was time to leave, we walked out of the restaurant to the sound of sirens in the distance. I thought, "What was that all about?"

Natalie

Chloe and the Italian Connection

Chapter 1

The taxi arrived to take us home. Natalie and I got in the taxi. I told him where to go, and he said that we could not go there, as there had been some type of explosion. I said to take us as close as possible.

We got out of the taxi at the roadblock. We asked the police officer what had happened, and he said that there had been an explosion in a flat. I said that we lived in no. three. "Is it OK to go through?"

The explosion had come from flat three.

Natalie started crying. She sobbed and said that her whole life was in the flat. The police officer said that the fire department and bomb squad were present, and all the flats had been evacuated. He advised us to get a hotel or to stay with friends.

Natalie phoned Chloe, and she said that we could stay in her spare room for the night.

The taxi was still parked there, and we asked them to take us to Chloe's house. Natalie sobbed in Chloe's arms, and she took her inside. Paul, Chloe's husband, invited me in. He had not come to the party, and did not look happy.

Natalie calmed down and sat with me. She sobbed, "Why has the best night of my life been ruined."

I kissed her, and said, "At least we were not at home and we are both safe. I love you so much."

Chloe started crying then, and gave us both a cuddle. Paul asked if the police knew what had happened. I just said that there had been a bomb and did not know anything else. Paul turned on the TV. There it was, on News 24, about an explosion in Chelmsford.

We went to bed, and I cuddled Natalie. I don't think any of us slept a wink all night.

Susan was at home by now. I don't know why they thought I was Colin's wife. I am his twin sister. I got revenge on them for Colin. I do hope that they were both in the flat. I used Colin's duplicate key to get into the flat. I used a small timer bomb and placed it under the table to go off Saturday evening.

We thanked Paul and Chloe, they lent us some clothes, and we got a taxi to our flat. Chloe was a bit larger than Natalie, so the clothes were not her usual figure-hugging style. She still looked stunning. Natalie would make a sack look good.

The road was still blocked off, but we were allowed through to be interviewed by the police. They asked loads of questions about where we were the previous night, and the rest of our movements over the last few days. They suggested that we get away for a few days away from the area.

I rang Steve to tell him what had happened as the flat was in the company name. I said we needed to get away from Chelmsford for a few days. Steve said Caroline would be able to run the office for a few days while we were away. Natalie and I both agreed that she was the perfect choice and would probably take over when Natalie and I left. It would be a good experience for her.

I said that we have to do some shopping, as we have lost everything at the moment, and to come down to Tunbridge Wells for a while. Our cars were still safe in the rear car park, so Natalie drove her car around to Chloe's. She got in mine, and we drove down towards Tunbridge Wells.

Chapter 2

We stopped off at Lakeside for Natalie to buy a brand-new wardrobe. The smile was re-appearing back on Natalie's face. We drove down to my apartment that actually was in a small village outside Tunbridge Wells, called Horsmonden. Natalie adored my apartment. It was part of a new build two years ago. I was able to buy it outright with money to spare, most of which was inherited from my parents. Natalie was beaming and said, "I love it here. I want this to be our home when we get married." I did not know it was possible to love Natalie even more than I did. She had made it so easy for me, as that was what I really wanted as well.

It was getting late now, so we quicky showered and changed. Natalie had bought this gorgeous dress, tied at the waist just below knee length with a split on the right side. She looked absolutely stunning, and I told her so. We walked to the pub in the village to have a meal. I knew a lot of the people in there. They all gasped when they saw Natalie. Pete said, "Who is this lovely lady?" I held up Natalie's hand to show them the ring.

I said, "this beautiful young lady is Natalie, my fiancé." Pete shook my hand and said it was about time.

"Would you like a table for food?" He said he was sorry that there was not a full menu tonight, as it was a Sunday night. We said that was OK.

Natalie sat at the table and thought that village life was what she had always dreamed of. This was so perfect.

We had our meal, one too many drinks, and walked home to

the apartment, went to bed, made love, and slept like logs.

It was Monday morning, and we had laid in until ten a.m. I can't remember the last time that had happened.

I brought Natalie a cup of coffee in bed. She looked so beautiful, even first thing in the morning. I said, "Come on. We need to do some food shopping, or we will starve."

She gulped down her coffee and said, "Race you to the bathroom." I let her win, and we had a wonderful shower together.

I said, "I love you."

Natalie replied, "I bet I love you more."

We got dressed and drove to the supermarket in Paddock Wood, went back home, stored all the food, and drove to the head office in Tunbridge Wells. There was a traffic jam. So, we were sitting there, and Natalie suddenly said, "How many children are we going to have?" I said I would love to have two little Natalie's running around. She smiled and said that she always wanted two as well.

We arrived at the Tunbridge Wells Branch and went straight to Steve's office. He said congratulation with a beaming smile. I knew it all along. I said, "Did you set us up?"

He said, "Sort of; I had a hunch." Natalie and I both said thank you at the same time.

Down to business then. The police had been in touch as the property was owned by the company. They said that a small bomb had been planted under the table. It had destroyed most of the lounge/dining area, but the bedrooms and bathroom were pretty much intact. I looked at Natalie and you could see some of the relief on her face. Steve continued. However, it looks like you two were the targets. They found some fingerprints and it appears that they were from a lady called Susan Bloom. She was posing as Colin's wife, but was really his twin sister. We both gasped and said, "Has she been caught?"

Steve added. Not yet, but they want you both to stay here until she is found. Natalie said, "What about my car, it is parked around Chloe's house. Does that put them in danger?"

Steve picked the phone up and contacted the police. They were sending a car there now. Five minutes later, Steve's phone rang. It was the police. They had found two bodies at the house. They were being taken to the hospital as we spoke. They did not know if they were alive or dead.

Chapter 3

Chloe and Paul were lying in bed, Sunday night, and were arguing. Paul was angry. "Why did you let them stay with us? Not only that. Her car is parked in the drive." Chloe was crying.

Natalie had become her best friend since starting work at the office. She had shared in confidence that her marriage was over, and they were just going through the motions. Chloe had been told she could not have children. When she told Paul, he went quiet and went to the pub and got so drunk. He came back home and beat up on Chloe, saying, "Don't you dare say that you want to adopt a child."

Chloe was scared after that, but covered it up so well when she was at work. No one else knew about it. Natalie had kept it a secret for her, but so wanted her to report it to the police. She started going to the gym with Natalie, and had lost weight. She was starting to get her youthful figure back. Paul resented her friendship with Natalie, but Chloe was past caring. Paul had lost his job for punching someone at work. He was just moping about at home doing nothing, then going out drinking in the evening.

This was the last straw for Chloe. She got out of bed, and packed her bags to leave Paul. He was trying to stop her and hit her so hard that she collapsed on the floor unconscious. They were in the lounge and the doorbell rang. Paul thought, *I hope it's not those two coming back.* He opened the door and stood facing Susan who was pointing a gun at him.

She told him to step back. She came in and closed the door.

"Where are they?" she said.

"They are not here, Susan."

Chloe had come round, and said, "Susan, you know each other?"

Paul laughed, and said, "We have been lovers since I lost my job. I was even round there when Alan was looking for Colin."

"Yes," Susan said. "You are just a lazy loafer."

Paul suddenly looked angry and went for the gun. She shot him in the chest. Chloe tried to run, but Susan shot her as well. Susan picked up Natalie's car keys and drove her car away.

Chapter 4

Natalie stood up and said, "We have to go back."

Steve and I said, "NO."

"Susan is obviously looking for us. She may know where the head office is, but not where I live." Steve nodded in agreement.

Natalie said, "OK, but I need to tell you something. I promised Chloe I would not tell anyone, but I think you need to know.

"Chloe and I became friends almost from when I started six months ago. She was very bubbly and friendly, and I took to her right away. I could also see that something was troubling her. I invited her to join me in the gym after work and got a six-month membership for her as she said they did not have any money.

"We got talking a lot and she confided in me that her husband Paul had been beating her after drinking sessions. I told her to report him; I even said I would go with her.

"She just seemed too afraid to do it. Gym night after work became a regular thing, and Chloe had lost over a stone in weight. It made her look like a young girl again. She also said that she had been to a specialist who said that she could not have children."

Just then Steve's phone rang. It was the police. They said that Paul was dead, and that Chloe was in a critical condition following a gunshot wound. Steve said we had some information and passed the phone to Natalie. She relayed what she had told us.

They advised us to stay here and be vigilant in the Tunbridge Wells office. I said, "We will, and gave them our cell phone contact numbers."

Natalie then said, "Wait. You said Susan stole my car. It is fitted with a tracker, and I can trace it on my phone." Natalie loaded the app, and saw that her car was travelling down the A21. She gave the police the tracker details so they could track it as well.

Steve said, "You had better go home until further notice, in fact, take two weeks paid leave. Neither of you have had a holiday in years."

We drove back to the apartment. Unusually, Natalie was very quiet.

We arrived home and I asked her what was wrong. She started crying in my arms. She said, "It is because of us that this poor girl is fighting for her life."

I said, "of course it is not. It is Susan and Colin's fault."

She calmed down and said, "I love you so much."

I said, "I love you too." We sat cuddling in silence for a while. I know she was thinking about Chloe.

Natalie jumped up suddenly and went over to my CD collection. She gave a little scream and said, "I don't believe it. You like all my favourite artists." She picked out a CD and put it on.

Whitney Houston's voice came on, singing 'I Will always Love You'. She took my hand and we danced around the room. Natalie started singing along. Natalie had an amazing voice and could sing it perfectly.

"Is there anything you can't do?"

She said, "it must be the Italian in me."

After it had finished, I got my laptop out and searched the local entertainment. I found what I wanted. Natalie squinted her eyes and said, "What are you up to?"

I said, "A surprise."

"Am I going to like this surprise?"

I said, "I hope so."

I said that I would cook dinner, Natalie wanted us to do it together. We managed a great meal together after having a flour fight.

"OK, get yourself showered and dressed up. We are going out later." She flashed me her beautiful smile and dashed off to the bathroom.

Natalie was getting excited and was pestering me about where we were going. I was not going to tell her, or she might change her mind.

I pulled into a pub just outside Tunbridge Wells. You could hear singing coming from inside.

I led her inside, and she then she realised it was a karaoke bar. I bought Natalie a large wine and a coke for me as I was driving. We found a seat and listened to people singing or not singing, whatever was the case. They then called up Natalie to sing. She turned to me and said, "I can't do this."

I said, "You will be amazing." I led her up the microphone. I said, "Look at the screen," and backed away. The intro to 'I will Always Love You' started. Natalie took a deep breath and started singing.

The bar went silent as everyone was now looking at my beautiful Natalie, listening to her wonderful voice. When she finished, the whole bar stood up, cheering and clapping, shouting for more. She shyly said, "Maybe another one later."

She walked back where we were siting to the chant of

'Natalie, Natalie.' She was suddenly really excited, and loads of people came up and asked what show she was in. Had she done the 'Bodyguard'? She just kept saying she had never sung in public before. You could see Natalie had never received this sort of attention before. An hour later, they called Natalie's name again, and this time she was cheered all the way to the microphone. She sang 'My Heart Will Go On' by Celine Dion. Again, she had a standing ovation and chanting for more. The end of the evening came too soon. I wanted Natalie to sing more, but everyone had to take their turn.

Natalie was singing in the car all the way home. It was beautiful. When we got in, Natalie gave me such a big kiss and thanked me for making her do this. I said, "You do not know how good you are. I had an agent come up to me when I went up to the bar for a drink, asking me if you wanted to sing professionally." Natalie looked shocked. She said that night was great fun, but she liked her job better.

Natalie thought for a minute, then got up and loaded up my laptop. I want to show you something. She loaded a picture of an Italian girl and showed me. My jaw dropped. It could have been Natalie's twin sister, only slightly younger. I said, "Who is that?"

"She is Benedetta. I would like to name our daughter that if we had one." I was not going to argue with that.

I smiled and said maybe we try a little bit tonight. She jumped up, and giggled, "Take me to bed, lover." Natalie said that she wanted a baby right away as we were a bit older. The way we were going, it would have happened sooner rather than later.

Chapter 5

Detective Stan Cooper was pondering how a jealous beating had turned into a house bombing, an attempted murder and a murder. Fortunately, Susan had been stopped just outside Tunbridge Wells and was in police custody. The good news was that Chloe had been moved out of intensive care and would be woken up later that day.

He was sure that there was much more to this case, and he wanted to speak to Natalie about her family history. He rang us saying that he would be down this afternoon.

Natalie and I rose early and we went for a run in the country lanes. We both had neglected our normal fitness regime since we had met. I was amazed at how easily Natalie kept up with me. I did wonder if I was actually slowing her down. I had put a chicken casserole in the slow cooker before we left. The smell when we walked back in was wonderful. We went in the shower together and I thought, *This girl is unbelievable.* I did not want it to ever end. After a light lunch, we met detective Cooper at the police station. We had packed our new gym gear for afterwards.

He said the good news first. "Chloe is out of intensive care. Her parents have been sitting with her."

Natalie said, "Can I go back and see her?"

He said, "Not just yet. Can you give me any background on your family?

Natalie knew a lot about her father, but she only knew her mother came from Italy. He took a deep breath and said that did she know that her parents' car crash was very suspicious, but there was not enough evidence to prove anything. It almost looked like a professional hit.

Natalie looked at me in disbelief. She had thought it was just a car crash.

She put her head in her hands and starting sobbing, saying, "OMG." I went and cuddled her.

I looked at the detective and said, "Did you really have to tell her that? She has already been through a lot."

He said he was sorry, but really needed to know about the Italian connection. Natalie nodded. She said if it was really a hit, she would do anything to help bring the people to justice.

Detective Cooper said that what we want could be dangerous for both of us. I said it had been that since we met in Chelmsford. I thought, *What is buried deep in Natalie's past that someone would want to harm her?*

I asked how the interrogation of Susan was going. He said, "Not well. She is not talking until she gets a lawyer. She insisted on it being one from Italy. He arrives at Gatwick this afternoon."

We looked at each and said in unison, "From Italy."

I asked if Susan and Colin were from Italy then. He said no, but their father was Italian. Natalie could not tell him anymore, but said they were welcome to study any documents from her bedroom in the flat. He thanked us and we left.

We went to the gym and signed Natalie up for a six-month membership.

Natalie put me to shame in the gym. She was working off all her frustration on the poor equipment. The instructor offered her a job on the spot. It made Natalie smile, so she was feeling better.

We went back home, showered, and put on some music. We just sat there cuddling each other, kissing occasionally. She did not sing along this time. She suddenly said, "We need to get organising this wedding." I said that I couldn't wait. "Let us make it tomorrow's task for the day."

"Make time for a run, the gym and love-making," she said.

I replied, "OK, let's start now." After we had cleared up the meal, Natalie said she was tired and wanted to go to bed. She lied – we did not go to sleep for ages. What had I awoken?

Natalie was laying half awake. Something had been troubling her; she thought things had changed when Alan came on the scene. Well, they did, they had fallen hopelessly in love. That was not it, because when Colin first started work, he was sort of OK. Then he changed. It was before Alan had arrived. Natalie must have dozed off, because she suddenly woke with a start.

She said, "I have got it. I know what this is all about." She turned to me and kissed me. She rushed into the lounge and fired up my laptop. She loaded up YouTube and started playing 'I Will Always Love You', sang by Benedetta. I suddenly woke up properly and sat and watched it with her. Her and Natalie sounded almost the same, looked the same and had the same amazing figure.

I said, "OK, so she is your double."

Natalie said, "She is more than that, but I did not realise until just now. Colin changed when he walked in my office one day on my lunch break; I was playing this video and his face changed. From that point he started his pestering campaign. I don't know how, but I believe Benedetta is my sister."

Natalie

Benedetta

Chapter 1

Natalie thought, *It is all coming back to me now. When I was twelve, Mum and Dad went away. I was left with my nan and grandad for six months while they visited family in Italy. I remember being so upset that they did not take me with them. I think that was what gave me a complex and made me feel so unloved. When Mum and Dad returned, I was constantly crying. Five years ago, Mum so wanted to go back to Italy. Dad gave in, and they were on the way to the airport when they were killed.* It all made sense now.

When we got up in the morning, Natalie told me her theory.

We rang detective Cooper in the morning, and he agreed that it was all beginning to make sense.

Detective Cooper sat at his desk, typing notes from what Natalie had said. His theory had been correct all along. Colin and Susan need to be re-interrogated with this new information. They both looked really scared now, and clammed up totally.

He then contacted Interpol to see if they knew anything about Colin and Susan. Also, if there was any information about Benedetta's family.

Stan's mind drifted to the beautiful, young, blonde woman lying in the hospital bed. How could anyone hurt such a lovely person? I need an excuse to interview her again. I will have to ask her on a date when she gets better. *He then felt depressed again, as every relationship he had fell through because of his* work. Stan pulled himself together and thought of the blue-eyed blonde in the hospital.

It looked like a big weight had been lifted from Natalie now. She started singing as she demanded to give the apartment a spring clean. "When did you last do this?" she said.

"My life is not going to be as easy as I thought," I chuckled. "Come on, let's go for this run."

She took the lead this time, and pushed me to the limit to keep up. When we got back, she had an enormous grin on her face. "You're out of condition, Alan. Come on, let us shower." We showered and we sat down with a cup of tea. I had not seen her drink tea before. Another surprise. She came over and gave me a kiss and a 'thank you'. "Without you I would never have worked this out or I may even be dead." She kissed me very passionately this time. "I love you so much." The cheeky grin returned, and she said, "I am late with my period, and I am always on time." I picked her up and spun her around, saying 'I love you' over and over again.

I looked into Natalie's gorgeous brown eyes and said, "You are the most beautiful woman I have ever seen. I feel like the luckiest man in the world."

Natalie said, "I think that I am the lucky one, my handsome, dark-haired, blue-eyed man. I love you. Please don't say anything to anyone until I do a test."

"Let us start organising this wedding then." She said that she wanted it in Chelmsford, as all her friends were there.

We had some good news that Chloe was recovering well. In fact, she rang us, and I am sure Natalie told her that she had missed her period. I heard loads of giggling and whispering on the phone.

Chloe rang Natalie's mobile and chatted with her friend who she had not seen since she left for Kent. Natalie could not help but tell her friend that she was very late with her period. Chloe wished she could give her friend a big hug.

Chloe had some news as well. "That nice detective did some research into the so-called specialist that said I could not have children was a fraud."

She said, "I really think Stan likes me."

Natalie thought, Stan is it, *and a lot of giggling was going on. Chloe said that she thought he was going to ask her on a date when she got better. Natalie said, "Do you want to?"*

Chloe replied, "Oh, yes."

Natalie said, "You know that YouTube video I am always looking at? I think that Benedetta could actually be my sister."

I told her to get Chloe to check out the specialist report. I thought it all looked suspicious, that Chloe was unable to have children. Natalie shouted back, "Already done, the specialist was a fraud."

I suggested that we go for a walk, as there were some beautiful fishing lakes about a mile up the road. We walked slowly with our arms around each other continually chatting. Natalie told Alan about detective Stan and Chloe.

Natalie and Alan arrived at the fishing lakes. They stopped for a soft drink and sandwich. "I love this place," said Natalie and we kissed again. We walked back slowly taking the scenery in.

"What shall we do for dinner?"

Natalie said, "Why not go out tonight? I saw a lovely pub on the way to the Karaoke bar. If we go early, we can also drop in there later."

"You have got the bug," I teased her. She said she was so scared at first, but then really enjoyed it after. I said, "Bring your earplugs, because I may have a go as well."

She looked at me and said, "Really?"

Chapter 2

We quickly got showered and changed. Natalie put on a lovely dress she had for the engagement party. I thought, *I know what all the male eyes are going to be looking at tonight.*

We had a light meal as the menu was disappointing.

We arrived at the karaoke bar at about eight p.m. Natalie said, "just a diet coke for me, please." I came back with a diet coke and a lager.

I said, "if you are not drinking then you are driving."

I was terrified at singing especially as Natalie was so good. It was a quiet night, and I was called up first. Oh no. Natalie got her revenge and pushed me up to the microphone. I had put in a country song 'O lord it's Hard to be Humble' by Mac Davis. Natalie said she had never heard it before. If you have never listened to the song, it was a comedy song, and Natalie was laughing all the way through it. It went down well with the crowd, but I knew they were waiting for Natalie.

Natalie was called up next and sang 'I Wanna Dance With Somebody' by Whitney. The crowd just would not let her get off the stage afterwards. She had to sing three more songs before they let her go. The chanting of 'Natalie' went on for ages and no one wanted to follow her. The host had to sing a couple of songs to keep the evening going. I did not get up again, but Natalie did one more song. 'The First Time Ever I Saw Your Face' by Roberta Flack. It was so emotional that I don't think there was a dry eye inside the place. Everyone kept cheering for more. I was so proud of her.

The talent scout came and sat at our table and was pleading with Natalie to do a professional gig on her own. Natalie was so taken aback by what had happened I could see she was tempted. She took his card anyway to please him. Natalie drove my car back home even though I had only one pint, and said to me, "Honestly, do you think I am good enough to sing on my own for an evening?"

I said, "you are one of the best singers I have heard in my life. You saw the reaction from the crowd. It was not just because you are beautiful; you can really sing."

We were really tired, and for the first time in ages went straight to sleep.

Natalie woke in the night and had been dreaming about being a singer. She thought that if Benedetta could do it, maybe she could as well.

In the morning, Natalie was scrolling through Facebook and suddenly jumped up saying Benedetta was coming to London.

Natalie picked up the phone and rang detective Cooper. He answered from the hospital. He said, "Hello, Miss James." Natalie told him about Benedetta coming to London, but he already knew. He said, "Can you and Alan come back to Chelmsford?" as he needed to talk in private. He said come in Alan's car as he believed Natalie's car had more than one tracking device in it. Natalie said they would drive straight to the police station.

Stan ended the call to Natalie and went back to Chloe's bedside. He was quiet for a while with a worried look on his face, so Chloe asked him what was wrong. Stan decided to bite the bullet; he went and closed the door to the private room, sat down beside Chloe and said, "Will you go on a date with me when you get better? I know this is very unprofessional, but I just had to ask." Chloe could see that Stan was very nervous, so she just laid quietly for a moment pondering. Don't tease him anymore, just say yes. So, she said, "Yes, I would love to." You could see the relief on Stan's face.

He smiled, and said, "You had better get well quickly, then." He looked at the pretty, blue-eyed blonde and thought, How could someone treat you so badly?

Chapter 3

Natalie and Alan arrived at the police station and went to see detective Cooper. He said, "Sit down, I have some news for you."

Natalie chuckled. "Yes, you have asked Chloe on a date." Stan blushed for a second, but recovered quickly. Natalie smiled at him and said it was OK. "Chloe needs someone nice in her life."

Stan thought, *I like this woman.*

"OK," he said. "Back to business. It seems that Benedetta's parents are not really her real parents. Benedetta had an accident and needed a blood transfusion. Benedetta is blood type 'O+', the same as you and your mother. Benedetta's parents had to own up about buying her illegally on the black market, as their blood types are 'AB+' and 'A+' respectively. Benedetta knows this, but still calls them her mum and dad.

"It looks like a lot of money was paid to your mum and dad at that time. That is why you inherited a large amount of money. We would like you to do a DNA test and meet with Benedetta and ask if she will do the same. We can't force her, so you will have to tread carefully. I feel confident that you are right and she is your sister.

"Benedetta does not know about you, so it is going to be quite a shock for her. She has a boyfriend travelling with her. We are not sure about him, as his past appears to have been erased. We are strongly thinking there is a Mafia connection here. Interpol agrees. We want Alan to go with you. Arrangements have been made to meet her. There will be plain clothes police, who will be armed, there to protect you just in case."

Natalie looked at me, and said, "Interpol, Mafia?"

I said to Natalie, "are you sure you want to do this? I could not bear anything happening to you."

Natalie did not hesitate and said, "yes, I will do it."

Chapter 4

"Benedetta's parents are worth over five hundred million euros, but she does not appear to be interested in the fortune. She is very intelligent and has her degree in economics. The same as you two. She is more interested in her singing career. Natalie, you are engaged now, so you need to talk to Alan." He looked at me and said, "You need to come clean with Natalie." She looked at me with a stern look.

I said, "it looks like we both need to talk about our past now. I have been hesitant, as it has not gone well in the past."

Stan said, "stay here and talk. I will close the door. I have a pretty blonde to interview," he said with a big grin on his face.

Natalie said, "I love you so much and I don't want to lose you." She took a deep breath and spoke. "I am actually worth over ten million pounds. It was inherited from my parents. I still own my parents' house as I did not have the heart to sell it. A large part of the money is invested in this company, and I am a silent partner. Stan is the only one who knows who I am. When people find out they normally want me for the wrong reasons."

I put my head in my hands and Natalie suddenly looked horrified. I said it was OK, and such a relief.

My turn. "I am worth over hundred million pounds. My father was a very successful merchant banker. He did not die of cancer, but a massive heart attack.

"I still believe his death was very suspicious. My mother did really die of cancer. I did not want that life for me. Every time a girl found out about my fortune, they also wanted me for the wrong reasons. My life has been so lonely until I met you, and I am so relieved you are not after my money.

"I also am a silent partner and the major shareholder in this company. Stan does not know that, so I will have to come clean with him."

Natalie jumped up and kissed me. "How do you know I am not after your money? You have more than me." She grinned.

"I would exchange it all to have you for the rest of my life."

She said, "you don't have to."

We did not realise how long we had been talking because Stan walked back in the room. "We have to move now," he said. "Benedetta is in London now and is preparing to shoot a video. We are delaying things and have the so-called boyfriend otherwise detained." We got in the police car and sped off, sirens wailing. Benedetta was in Hyde Park waiting to shoot her video. Why do we have a technical problem? This has never happened before.

Natalie and I were standing behind her, and Natalie said, "Hello, Benedetta." We made her jump; she turned round and looked in shock. She was every bit as beautiful in real life. Her pictures did not do her justice. Natalie held out her hand and said, "Hi, my name is Natalie. I saw your YouTube videos and could not believe how we looked so alike. We sound very similar when we sing as well."

Benedetta sat down and spoke English with a slight accent. "You look just like an older version of me," Natalie said, and pointed to me. "This is my fiancé, Alan. May I have a private chat with you?"

I let them walk together and they chatted. They returned in a while, and they were holding hands. "We are going to do a duet together." Miraculously, the equipment started working, and they sang 'I Have Nothing' together.

"I need to use this on my channel," she said.

Natalie said, "OK, but not just yet. Will you do the DNA test? I just have to know."

"Oh, yes," she said, "so do I." We had a medic with us, and she quickly took a sample.

Chapter 5

Just then, her boyfriend turned up.

"What is going on here?" he said.

"Hi, Giorgio, this is Natalie and Alan. We have just recorded a video together."

Giorgio said, "No, you can't be seen together." He pushed Natalie out of the way and was going to snatch Benedetta's camera when I stepped in front of him.

"You do not push my fiancé like that, or any other lady for that matter."

He pulled a gun on me. Benedetta screamed at him. "Giorgio, what are you doing?"

"You two cannot be seen together, they will realise that you are sis…" He stopped speaking, but it was too late.

I said, "You mean sisters."

He said, "Move out of the way and give me the camera."

Benedetta said no, and put the gun away. "So, we really are sisters." Giorgio got angry and raised the gun up.

"Drop that weapon," came the shout from behind him. Giorgio turned, I then kicked the gun out of his hand and Stan wrestled him to the ground.

Natalie said, "Is that your boyfriend?"

Benedetta said, "Oh, no, he is the horrible bodyguard they sent to protect me. I hate him, he is always so horrible." She said something in Italian to him.

Giorgio said, "you are all dead now, me as well."

Stan said, "you can tell us all why then."

"Not talking to you," he said.

"You can talk to Interpol then, and never see daylight again." They police hauled Giorgio away and left us together.

Natalie looked at Benedetta and they rushed into each other's arms. "Are we really sisters?" Benedetta asked.

Stan reappeared and said, "It looks that way, the DNA test will just confirm it. How is this possible? How come I did not know I had a sister?"

Natalie said, "neither did I until a couple of days ago."

"Will you all come to the station for a talk? We will fill you in on the whole story."

We sat in the station and Stan filled Benedetta in on what had happened. She asked if her parents involved in all this. Stan said, "The only thing we are 100% sure of is that they paid Natalie's parents for you."

"Why?" she said.

Stan replied, "we strongly believe that Natalie's and your parent's family had been under threat to do it. They were paid a lot of money for it and to keep their silence. An Italian Mafia family appear to be behind this. That is why there is a big threat. If it is OK with you Benedetta, we can put you up in a safe house for a couple of days to let Interpol do their job."

Benedetta agreed, but was worried about her things at the hotel.

Stan organised everything and we went to the safe house. I left the girls to sit and talk; they had a lifetime to catch up with, after all.

I went and found detective Cooper. "How long do you think we have to stay here?"

"Not long, I hope."

"So how is Chloe?"

His eyes lit up at the sound of her name. "She is doing so well and is likely to be released tomorrow. I need to get her someplace safe as well as she is a possible target."

"That is good, and I trust you to look after her. She is a special girl."

He said, "I know."

There was a knock on the door. It was the DNA result. A 60% match. That is above average for sisters. That was it, congratulations, girls. I went over and hugged them both. They started crying with happiness. How often in life do you get a present like that?

"Don't you have a pretty blonde to take care of Stan?"

He said yes and left them together with a police guard outside. We sat down and watched the girls singing together. It was amazing.

I said, "That is it, we need to get you both into a recording studio and record an original song."

Benedetta said she had written over thirty songs. The girls went through the songs while I went for a walk with one of the detectives to stretch my legs. When we returned the police, guard was laying on the floor unconscious. We dashed into the room and saw the two girls sitting and tied up in chairs. With guns pointing at them.

Natalie

Chloe's Recovery

Chapter 1

"Come in slowly with your hands in the air," one of them said. We obliged. I looked at Natalie and I could see she was scared. Benedetta was sobbing under her gag, tears rolling down her beautiful face.

I said, "what do you want?"

The same one said, "Sit over there." We slowly moved to the two chairs. At least they were looking at us now.

The door burst open and four armed police poured into the room and shot both of the men. They dropped instantly to the ground. I rushed over to free Natalie and Benedetta. They embraced each other sobbing their hearts out. When they calmed down, I hugged them both and asked what had happened. Natalie said that soon after we left the two men burst into the room tied them up and gagged them. "We were so scared as they were waving the guns at us threateningly wanting to know where you were."

"Me?" I said. "Why me?" They did not know.

Detective Stan returned and said that they were just hoods trying to hold me for ransom. I said, "Who were they going to ask for the ransom money?" It did not make sense. Stan looked puzzled as well.

"It is a good job we had surveillance cameras in here."

"I am not happy here; can we just go back to my apartment? Benedetta can come as well." She nodded in agreement.

Stan said, "OK. We will take you back to your car and drive

down there without police. I think we may have a mole."

We drove back home. The two girls sat in the back talking, catching up on their lives. I stopped to pick up a Chinese and noticed a car had been following us. I rang Stan and he said it was him. He wanted to know we got home OK. I said, "Thanks, do you want some Chinese?" He said no thanks as he was just about to turn back as someone was being discharged from hospital in the morning. I said goodnight, and thought, *There is a good guy.*

We arrived back home and tucked into the Chinese with a few glasses of wine. Benedetta had recovered now, but I could see she was tired. I said, "you sleep in my bed tonight with Natalie and I will sleep on the couch."

She said no, but Natalie said it was OK. "You go and shower and I will join you later."

Natalie and I sat on the three-seater couch together. I said, "You were wonderful today, and so brave."

"I did not feel it," she said.

I gave her a kiss and said, "You had better join Benedetta in bed. I think we all need a good night's sleep tonight."

Natalie went in the shower, came out and gave me a kiss goodnight. She said, "I love you so much and now I have a sister to love as well."

I said, "I love you and will miss you tonight." She slid off to the bedroom. I sorted out some bedding for the couch and went in the shower. I came out and someone was already on the couch. It was Benedetta.

She said, "Please sleep in your own bed with my sister. It is not fair as you have done so much for me already." Bless her; I gave her a peck on the forehead said good night and joined Natalie in my bed.

She turned over and said, "Hello, my wonderful lover."

I woke up to the sound of girls chatting. They were already up and dressed and had a cup of coffee ready for me. "Come on, lazybones, time for a run."

"What time is it?" I looked at the clock and saw it was only seven a.m. I put on my running gear and joined the girls. I could see they were going to give me a workout that day. I now had double trouble, but they took it easy on me and we finished up at the fishing lakes. We ordered breakfast. Scrambled egg on toast, and it was perfect. We walked back to the apartment. We took it in turns to shower and I rang Stan to find out what was happening.

He said no one was talking. The two that were shot by the police were recovering in hospital under armed guard.

They were running the DNA tests again. There results were actually higher than what they said. It was actually a 100% match, which would make them identical twins. Which was impossible. "Don't tell the girls yet."

Chapter 2

Lorenzo and Sofia Romano were getting worried as they had not heard from Benedetta in two days. It was unusual, as she always rang them every day when she was away from home. That horrible bodyguard, Gorgio, could not be contacted either. Why did we agree to let Tommaso talk us into hiring him?

They lived on the beautiful island of Lampedusa, which is part of the Pelage Island group in the Mediterranean Sea. In fact, they owned most of the Island. They were both sixty-three years old now. They bought Benedetta when they were forty as they realised Sofia could not have children.

Tommaso said that he could help them buy a baby, but it would be expensive. They had Benedetta given to them immediately after birth and raised her as their own. When Benedetta was fourteen, she had an accident and fell on a sharp rock. She was losing a lot of blood and needed a transfusion. That is when it came to light that they could not be Benedetta's parents. Benedetta was unhappy for weeks, but they were all she had ever known and of course loved them. She still called them Mum and Dad, but somehow things were different. She always thought something was missing in her life.

She graduated from University in England with a full honour's degree in economics. Benedetta was not interested in the family business, and only wanted to be a singer.

She created her own YouTube channel and started uploading cover songs. Her subscribers rocketed and was starting to get millions of views on her channel. She started travelling to different parts of the world recording her covers and uploading them to YouTube.

Tommaso was getting angry because Benedetta was too much in the limelight. We are going to get found out, *he thought.* He had already had to take care of Natalie's parents as they had started to find Benedetta and were coming to Italy to search for her.

Tommaso was a scientist in genetics and had devised a ground-breaking technique to split a fertilised egg. He paid for Natalie's parents to come to his clinic and carry out his procedure to make Natalie's mother pregnant. It worked perfectly and Benedetta was born. Then, Romano's paid Natalie's parents a lot of money for the child.

Over time, Natalie's mum and dad wanted Benedetta back. They had seen a girl singing on YouTube who looked just like a young Natalie. Tommaso had created a twin sister twelve years younger than the original. He was going to be in big trouble as the procedure was banned and had not worked before. He could not let the world find out. He used his mafia connections with the Zappa family to help him.

Chapter 3

Alan had the whole day planned out to amuse the girls.

Natalie called out, "What is this picture on the wall?" I panicked. By the time I got to the bedroom Natalie had taken the picture down, revealing my wall safe. She said, "What do you keep in there?" I said it was just some spare cash. She said, "OK, open it."

I thought, *why did I hang on to that stuff?* I opened the safe and took out a wad of cash and said, "There you are."

"What's that?" she said and grabbed the small box inside. She opened it and my heart sank. It was a ring. "What is this?" Natalie shouted. "Who is this for? And what is this 'Penny Brown'? You have been deceiving me all along." She was crying so bad.

"Natalie, please let me explain."

She ran out of the house and said, "Don't follow me." Benedetta asked what was wrong. "He is a cheat!" Natalie shouted back. Benedetta looked at me and asked what I had done.

"Let me at least explain to you."

Natalie was not listening.

Benedetta looked at me and then Natalie, not knowing what to do. I said, "Please." Tears were rolling down my cheeks. "Please."

She said, "OK, but my sister needs me right now."

I said, "Five years ago. I was in a relationship with Penny, which broke up. She came back three years later and said I was the father of her three-year-old son. The dates all tied up, so I believed her. I bought this to give the child a father. The apartment is still in her name. I came back early one day and found her in my bed with another man. We had a big row, and I had a DNA test done. I found that I had been tricked and I was not the father. As usual, I was being used. Benedetta, please talk to her. She won't listen. I have never loved anyone as I do Natalie." I was sobbing now. I went to my room. I had never been this down in my life.

Benedetta went outside and was talking to Natalie. She said, "Please go in and talk to Alan and let him explain."

Natalie said, "why? He lied to me." They sat together until Natalie calmed down.

Benedetta said, "do you love him?"

She said, "Of course I do, that is why I am so upset."

"Good. then let him explain. He did everything for the right reasons."

"Did he tell you everything?"

Benedetta said, "Yes. He is as distraught as you. Talk to him, I hate seeing you both this way."

"OK." Natalie said, "but please come with me."

They came back inside. I was sitting on the couch with my head in my hands, sobbing. Natalie went up to me and put her arms around me. She said, "I love you, Alan. Please tell me what this is all about."

I repeated what he said to Benedetta. I said, "Please forgive me, I think I only kept it all to remind me not to get cheated again. There are not anymore skeletons in the closet."

We both turned to Benedetta and said thank you. She gave us a hug and said, "I love you both."

Chapter 4

Stan went to the hospital to pick up Chloe. She was dressed and waiting. Stan said, "Wow, I knew you were pretty, but did not realise you were stunning."

Chloe giggled. "Come on, handsome detective. I am ready for this date now."

He said, "Not yet. We need to get you somewhere safe and get your strength back."

She teased and said, "You know how to let a girl down, don't you?"

He actually took her to his own house and showed her in the spare room. "this will be your room. You can use anything you wish while you are here."

Chloe put on a sad face. "So when am I leaving, then?"

Stan said, "Never if I can help it." He gave her a quick kiss on the lips. Chloe grabbed him and kissed him passionately.

"Like that in future or I am leaving." Stan was all weak in the knees. He had never been kissed like that before.

Stan recovered and said he had to go to work, but would check in later. "Don't forget to call me if there is a problem."

She grinned and said, "OK."

He went to the car and the phone rang. It was Chloe; she said, "I have a problem."

"What?" he said.

"You are not here," and she giggled.

Stan thought, This girl is going to get me in trouble. *He had* already broken a code of conduct for her.

The Interpol investigation was gathering pace, which was good. Stan could not get his head round why Alan was needed for Ransom. It could not have been about Natalie as they already had her at the time. It had to be something unrelated. He decided to reopen the investigation into Alan's father's death, as something was now niggling him.

I took the girls to Tunbridge Wells for some retail therapy and said I would meet them at the Gym in two hours. We all hugged goodbye, and they went off shopping for the first time together. They had big grins on their faces.

I went to the head office and went to see Steve. Steve greeted me with a big smile on his face. He said, "The builders are working on the flat in Chelmsford and will be finished in two weeks. Caroline is doing an excellent job running the office in their absence. So, what have you been up to?"

I said, "You know that anonymous investor?"

Steve nodded.

"Well, it is me."

Steve did not look surprised. He said he had an inkling that it was me. "You know, you and Natalie don't have to work at all if you don't want to."

I said it had been crossing my mind to do something different since Natalie and I got together. "Even more so now that Benedetta has come into our lives. No decisions yet, but have you heard them sing?"

He shook his head. I had brought the video they recorded in Hyde Park, and played it through his computer.

He said, "They are amazing; I can see where you are going with this."

I said, "Benedetta wants it, but Natalie is not sure. I think Benedetta is inspiring her. Thinking about those two, I left them doing some retail therapy."

"I am glad you are so happy," he said.

"I nearly blew it earlier. Natalie found the engagement ring I bought for Penny and documents in her name."

"OMG," he said, "how did you recover?"

"With a lot of help and understanding from Benedetta," I said. "Better go. We are meeting at the gym."

I only had to wait ten minutes before the girls turned up laden with bags. We signed Benedetta in as a guest member. The girls worked out together and were turning a lot of the male heads. I decided to do more weights than repetition this time.

We showered on the way out and the girls appeared in tight-hugging jeans and skimpy, light blue tops. They said, "Shall we go for an Italian meal first?" It was only a short walk. We had a fantastic meal.

I winked at Natalie to go to our favourite bar. "Too late," she said, "we have already decided to watch you sing tonight." Oh dear. I knew they were only joking.

Benedetta said, "Please call me Bene, all my friends do."

We went back home, and the girls changed again. They came out in really sexy, red dresses. They were going to kill it that night. Natalie said, "Don't worry. This all went on your card. Payback for this morning." She grinned.

"Good job I love you then."

The girls absolutely killed it on the stage that night, and you could see Natalie really gaining confidence. They sat in the back together on the way home, giggling and chatting like teenagers. When we got back, Natalie told us to sit down. She said, "I have some news. I am definitely pregnant." I was so happy.

Bene said, "A couple of days ago I did not know I had a sister, now I am going to be an auntie."

I said, "I have some news as well. The wedding is all booked for Saturday in ten days' time. You must stay for that, Bene."

"Do you think Chloe will be upset if she is not head bridesmaid? I now want Bene to do it. Give her a call in the morning."

Chapter 5

Chloe had been rummaging through the cupboards, fridge and freezer. She had found all the ingredient needed for her famous chicken pasta dish. She rang Stan to ask roughly when he would be home and started preparing. Stan walked in and said, "What is that lovely smell?" The table was laid out already with lighted candles and wine glasses.

"White or red?" she said. "I suggest White as it is chicken. Dinner in two minutes."

Stan could not believe this. The meal was delicious, and Chloe was such good company. "Well," she said, "what do you think of my cooking?"

"Amazing," he said, and meant it. "What is for dessert?"

She walked over, kissed him, and whispered, "Me."

He knew this was much too quick, but could not resist this gorgeous young lady.

They were laying in Stan's bed, and he said, "Why did we just do this?"

She said, "It has been a long time since anyone showed me they cared, and to be honest, I fancied you like crazy."

He said, "The feeling was mutual, but can we just take it steady? Please."

She said, "OK, but I am sleeping here from now on. If you don't like it, you can use the spare room," and kissed him. "That was fantastic, by the way."

No girl had ever said that to him before. Nor had he enjoyed sex as much before.

Chloe's phone ringing woke her up. It was Natalie. She looked and saw a note from Stan on the pillow.

See you later. I had to go into work early. XXX

She said, "Hi, Natalie, do I have some news for you, but you first."
"The wedding has been booked for Saturday week. Would you be upset if Benedetta was my main bridesmaid as it has been confirmed that she is my sister?"
Chloe said, "How could you do that to me?" She paused and said, "Only joking, of course, don't forget me, though."
"Of course not; what is your news?"
"I am living at Stan's and we had such amazing sex last night. He is so kind and thoughtful, not what I have been used to in the past."
Natalie said, "How did this happen?"
"He picked me up from the hospital yesterday and he stated that the only place he knew was safe was his house. He set me up in spare room and left me to fend for myself. I cooked him my famous chicken pasta dinner, lit some candles and drank wine. He said it was an amazing meal. When he said what is for dessert, I could not resist, kissed him and said 'me'. It's my fault. It just happened and it was so good."
Natalie said, "I am pleased for you, but just be careful, Chloe, you are very vulnerable at the moment. Oh, by the way, I am definitely pregnant."

Chapter 6

Stan rang soon after.

"Interpol have traced a lot of evidence to Tommaso Zappa. He has an experimental clinic on Sicily which is very dubious. The whole family have links to the Mafia. They would like the three of you to fly over there tomorrow to see Benedetta's family. Interpol cannot get to them as they have not done anything wrong. We need evidence that will link Benedetta and Natalie's parents to Tommaso. We think you may be able to get them to divulge the information needed."

I said, "Hang on, and I will put you on speaker so the girls can hear." I called them over and let Stan go through the plan. Bene said that she would not get her family in trouble, but they just needed a statement.

Bene said, "OK. I will arrange with Mum and Dad. And say that I have new friends with me one who can act as my bodyguard." She winked at me.

I said, "Is it safe?"

He said, "Interpol will be with us all the way. You will not even know they are there. We will leave as soon as possible for Chelmsford as Natalie and I need to pick up our passports at the flat."

Bene then rang her parent's and arranged everything with them. They were pleased to hear from her and delighted that she had sacked that horrible bodyguard.

Bene's parents booked the flight and we printed off the e-tickets. First class, of course. The flight was at 12.05 from

London Stansted to Rome, then a short flight from Rome to Lampedusa on the family private jet. I booked a family room at a Stansted hotel so we did not have to drive through the morning rush hour. I wanted us to stay altogether. Bene was quite happy with that.

This was going to be Bene's role now, as she was probably the only one who could talk her parents into testifying. Seeing Natalie would help as well. The flat repair was going well, and would be finished sooner than expected. Especially when I offered a large bonus for being finished by Wednesday next week.

Bene said, "you have a spare room here, so can I stay here before the wedding?" We said we would like that. We popped into the Chelmsford office before heading off to Stanstead. Caroline met us at reception. Chloe was there as well. She insisted on coming back part time for a while. Stan agreed only if he took her and picked her up.

Caroline was a bleached blonde in her forties. Short and slightly stocky. She had a very pleasant nature and ran the office like clockwork. The main thing was everyone liked her. Natalie could not resist. She said, "everyone, I am pregnant. Does that mean another party at that restaurant?"

I cleared my throat, and said, "my restaurant." Natalie looked quizzically at me. "How do you think I was able to book a venue so quick for the engagement party? How are the preparations going for the wedding?" Caroline had organised everything for us as well. "If this all goes to plan you deserve a raise."

I looked at Natalie and whispered, "We had better come clean soon." She nodded in agreement.

"No more secrets."

"Agreed."

Natalie

The Romano Family

Chapter 1

They landed at Lampedusa airport and was met by the family driver with the Limousine. "Hello Andrea," said Bene. "Are my parents at home?"

"Yes, miss, they are eagerly waiting to see you." It only took ten minutes to drive to the mansion. Bene led us inside while Andrea dealt with the luggage. "Mum, Dad, this is Natalie and Alan."

Sofia gasped. "How is this possible? She looks like your sister."

"That is because she is."

There was a short silence for everything to sink in. Sofia stuttered, "Wwwwhy, hhhow?"

"May we please sit down and tell you the whole story?" Natalie then stated that her parents, Bene's real parents, were killed while driving to the airport. They had seen Bene's YouTube video. Lorenzo had been very quiet.

"OK," he said, "how do we know you are sisters?"

"The DNA tests were 60% match."

I chirped in. "Actually it is 100%. You are twins." I had forgotten to tell them, so they all looked shocked.

"How can that be?" said Natalie. "I am twelve years older than Bene."

"How it is possible only Tommaso knows, but we believe he managed to split the fertilised embryo and freeze store it for twelve years, then reinsert it into your mother's womb. Scientist are saying it should not be possible. Interpol suspect he is doing something illegal. That is why they have tried to kill Natalie and also threaten Bene."

Lorenzo said, "wait here." You could hear him have an angry conversation with someone. "I am expecting a call back shortly."

Sofia said, "where do we stand on this, Bene? We never meant to hurt you." Bene went over and hugged her mother. Natalie went over also.

"I don't know you, but I would like to call you mother as well."

Sofia started to cry, saying, "I thought I was going to lose a daughter, instead I am gaining a daughter."

"Also, a son-in-law, as Natalie and I get married next week."

She turned to Lorenzo. "Do something about this or we are going to lose everything."

Lorenzo was furious; he was saying, "This is bad. We have family killing family. This is against everything we believe in. Tommaso has to pay for this."

Sofia called the butler. "Let us all have a drink – what would you like?" Fredrico took our order and returned shortly with coffee.

I was liking Lorenzo and Sofia. He made his money by starting his own shipping line from scratch, so he was a self-made man and definitely not a criminal. We had a lovely meal with them. The fish was superb. I must admit I was surprised when they gave Natalie and I a double room. Natalie telling them that she was pregnant may have something to do with that. I sent Stan a text.

Chapter 2

Stan and Chloe were watching TV when he received my text. He read it and said, "Great, things are going well."

Chloe said, "I am so glad as well. Are things going well here?" She winked at him. Stan smiled and gave her a big kiss. "That's better."

She had been saying earlier that she wanted to go back to the gym. Stan said, "NO. You need to build up slowly."

Chloe said she was getting flabby. Stan said, "What? You got to be kidding me. You are drop-dead gorgeous."

"So, you are not going to throw me out on the street, then?"

"Never," he said.

"Does that mean we are a couple then?"

"Yes, we are dating and sleeping together." He knew he was falling badly for Chloe. I hope she feels the same.

Chloe was thinking, I am in love with this man. I hope he feels the same soon.

Natalie and I woke early to the sun trying to pierce through the thick curtains. We made coffee with the machine in the room, showered and dressed. Natalie put on some skimpy shorts and a top showing her midriff off. I had shorts and tee-shirt. It was going to be a hot day.

We arrived down for breakfast. Sofia and Bene were sitting and chatting in Italian. They went back to English when we walked in. Bene said, with a massive grin on her face, "Good morning. How did you sleep?"

I said, "Like a log."

Sofia said, "Lorenzo has already left in the plane to Sicily. He will be back this evening."

Bene asked if we would like a tour of the island. "There are some amazing beaches as well, so bring your beachwear." Natalie pulled out a skimpy bikini from her pocket.

I looked in horror. "You are not wearing that, are you?"

She giggled and said, "Would you rather I went topless?"

Bene was wearing exactly the same outfit as Natalie. She pulled out a matching skimpy bikini. "Would you rather I went topless as well?" I was definitely in double trouble with these two.

Lampedusa was a truly beautiful island. I said to Natalie, "Shall we ask her now?"

Bene heard me. "What?" she said.

Natalie replied, "We would love to spend the first few days of our honeymoon here if it is OK."

Bene had an enormous smile on her face and jumped up and down like a kid. "I was hoping you would say that. I really want to get to know you both better. Not only that, we would love you to join us on the rest of the honeymoon around Italy." She was nearly crying now. "Are you sure?"

Natalie replied, "It's what we want. We love you, Bene, how could we not want you with us. You have twenty-three years to tell us about your life and I have thirty-five years to tell you about mine. If things had been left alone, we would have grown up together as identical twins. Life would have been so different."

I said, "I may not have had the chance to meet two of the most beautiful women on the planet."

Natalie said, "In that case, and we all met at Uni, which one of us would you choose?"

I said, "OK, then, which one of you would have had a crush on me?"

They looked at each other and said in unison, "Neither of us," and laughed. No way was I ever going to outwit these two.

I changed the subject and said, "So are you going to come with us? You can bring a boyfriend if you like."

Bene suddenly looked sad. "I don't have one," she said.

We both said, "Why not? You are so beautiful."

"There was a guy called Michael at Oxford I fell in love with. I really thought it was going to work out for us. I then found out he was seeing another girl. I was livid, I told him I did not want to see him again. A few days later he came up to me and said, 'Hi, Bene, meet Grace.' I slapped him and turned to Grace and said he has cheating on you with me. Don't trust him. Grace then slapped him. Grace and I became good friends at Uni after that. He got the two-timing reputation at Uni and no one else would go out with him."

Natalie said, "you dodged a bullet there, then."

She looked up with a tear in her eye and said, "but I still love him." Natalie comforted Bene as she sobbed quietly.

A thought suddenly struck me. "Was his name Michael Davenport?"

Bene looked up in shock. "How do you know?"

Natalie then got it as well. "We interviewed Michael Davenport to replace Colin in finance. When we asked him about any ties to the area as we might have needed him to move around, he said, 'No, I cheated on the girl I really loved at Uni'. She said that she never wanted to speak to him again. No one else could never replace her."

I was such a fool; I remembered how he gasped when he saw Natalie. Bene was silent and you could hear the gears turning in her head.

"I would like to meet him when we get back."

"I think we can arrange that." Natalie said.

When we got back to the Mansion, Lorenzo had returned and wanted a talk with us.

We walked into the lounge where there was a very sombre looking Lorenzo and Sofia. He said, "Please, sit down.

"It appears that Tommaso has been responsible for a lot of bad things." He looked at Bene and he said, "I am so sorry, but Tommaso used us as a part of one of his experiments. You and Natalie were twins in your mother's womb. Bene, you were separated from Natalie, removed, and freeze-stored. When we asked for a child, he paid your parents for the second part of the experiment. You were placed back in the womb and with his untried method managed to continue the pregnancy. It worked and you were born naturally. You were taken from your mother and Tommaso told them that you had not survived. You were then given to us for ten million euros."

What he had done was totally illegal and unethical. The experiment had never worked again afterwards, and Tommaso lost a lot of money. He was going to lose his clinic.

Five years earlier, two things had happened. Bene posted her first YouTube video. If Bene became famous, he would be found out for sure. Natalie or someone who knew Natalie would notice the likeness. He needed money fast.

He looked at Alan and said, "Your father was Frank Ford. Tommaso conned your father for a one hundred and fifty million investments in his clinic. He had forged documents that indicated ground-breaking medical developments including a cure for cancer. When this did not happen, your father lost all the money on the investment and had to pay it off to the investment company out of his own fortune.

"Before your father could start legal proceedings against Tommaso, he was injected with a drug to bring on a heart attack. He then had a call from Natalie's parents saying they were coming to Italy to find Benedetta. He then paid money to have your parents killed and to make it look like an accident. The families have outlawed Tommaso and seized all his assets. The one hundred and fifty million is going to be returned to you Alan. The families do not take kindly to people who kill their own. Tommaso has fled Italy with a couple of loyal supporters. Interpol have all this information with supporting documentation."

Lorenzo broke in tears and said, "Please forgive us, Benedetta. She rushed over into her fathers' arms. Natalie rushed over to Sofia who was also crying."

Alan went outside trying to take in how his father had been so easily conned. He thought, I am never going into banking. Natalie appeared and put her arms around Alan.

"I am so sorry that your father was involved in this as well." They sat on the bench with their arms around each other in silence.

Alan said that he should ring Stan and fill him in on the details. Natalie said, "OK and went to find her sister."

Bene asked, "How Alan was holding up?"

She said he would be OK. He was talking to Stan, filling him in on what we knew.

"We need a flight back tomorrow, are you coming, Bene?"

She looked at Sofia. "I am going to be a bridesmaid." Sofia

hugged her. "We can come back here after the wedding?" I did promise Alan and Natalie. Sofia looked at Lorenzo. He said they would be honoured to have her.

We boarded the private jet the next morning for Rome to pick up the next flight to Stanstead.

Natalie

The Wedding

Chapter 1

Stan walked in to an awesome aroma. Chloe had made a Stew and it was simmering away in the slow cooker.

"Hi," Chloe greeted Stan, and rushed from kitchen and gave him a welcoming kiss. Chloe was taken aback when Stan did not respond. "What is the matter? Have I done something wrong?"

"No," he said, "but you are going to."

"What am I going to do?"

"Leave," he said.

Chloe was nearly in tears now. She sobbed, "I am not going anywhere. Are you throwing me out?"

"No, but the case is nearly over, and you will go back home."

Chloe said, "Why would I do that? I am falling in love with you."

It was the answer he was hoping to get. He turned around and kissed her this time. "I am falling in love with you as well. Dinner will have to wait." He carried her up to the bedroom.

Michael Davenport was lying on his bed. He was dreaming about Benedetta and what a fool he had been. It was a shock at the interview. He thought it was her until he realised Natalie was an older version of Bene.

It had been frantic in the office with the upcoming wedding and being short staffed with Alan and Natalie being away. They looked so good together, and he was dreaming of Bene when they were dating. She used to sing to him in the bedroom. What a voice, *he thought*, she should go professional. *He thought*, She does not need the money. *Neither did he, as his father worked in the Stock Market.*

He unpacked his laptop and started playing her videos. She is so good. *He was wondering if she had a boyfriend and was in love. This depressed him, and he turned it off. He so wished he could have that day back and tell her how he really felt. He said to himself,* Michael, you are an idiot.

Bene was daydreaming on the plane. She was thinking about Michael and how good they were together. They had been dating for six months, and she decided to give herself to him. It was her first time, and it was wonderful. Michael was so kind and considerate. I was madly in love with him. *She could not get her head round it. She knows it could have been handled better, but she was devastated. She nearly left Uni to fly home. Fortunately, common sense kicked in.*

The captain said, "Fasten your seatbelts, please. We are on final approach to Stanstead." *She glanced over at Natalie and Alan. They had not stopped chatting the whole flight. They looked so happy together.*

Chapter 2

They landed and drove straight to the flat. It was almost finished. "Looks liveable," Alan said. The girls both nodded. "Let's get cleaned up and pop into the office."

Bene's heart missed a beat. *He is going to be there.* "Can I come?" she said. Alan and Natalie winked at each other.

Chloe greeted them with a hug. Caroline wanted to see both of us, so I sent Bene to my office. When she was out of sight, I went along to finance and said to Michael, "Can you please see me in my office?" He looked terrified.

"What is wrong, sir?" he said.

"You will find out." He followed me sheepishly. I opened the office door and said, "Bene, this is Michael Davenport. I have brought him to see you." I slipped out of the office and closed the door. There was a short silence.

Michael spoke first. "What are you doing here?" He put his head down and muttered, "Bene I am so sorry for what I did to you. I got scared and have regretted it for the last two years. I should not have done that to someone I loved."

Bene said, "I was so in love with you, and you hurt me so much. It was soon after that I realised that I still loved you, and have never stopped hurting."

"Does that mean you will take me back?"

Bene said, "No, but we can start over again."

Michael stepped forward and said, "May I kiss you?"

Bene leaned in and kissed him instead. "Sit down and let's talk."

"What about work?"

Bene said, "My sister is taking care of it. Yes," she said, "it is a very long story."

"It looks to be going well," Natalie said to me. "They just needed to be in the same room together." They walked out of the office to a smiling Natalie and I.

"You two planned this."

Natalie said, "Would you like to join us for an Italian in our restaurant?"

Michael looked at Bene and she nodded her head.

"See you there at seven, then. Let us go back and freshen up, Bene. You need a shower as well, Alan. Oh, and invite Stan and Chloe as well. I am dying for a catch-up."

I rang Stan – it went to answer phone, so I left a message. It rang back five minutes later. Stan was panting a bit. "Can you join us at seven p.m. at the Italian restaurant?"

"Well, Chloe has made a Stew."

Chloe shouted over him, "We are coming, see you there."

We had a lovely meal. Bene and Michael were getting on very well and Natalie did not stop talking all night. The band started up at nine p.m. and people were getting up and dancing. At ten p.m. I walked to the stage and talked to the band.

I picked up the microphone and said, "Welcome to my restaurant and Cabaret bar. Tonight, we have a special treat for you all. Welcome to the stage, Benedetta. Her videos have gained millions of views on YouTube."

Bene got up and walked to the stage. She said, "Please join me on the floor to dance to my favourite Whitney song."

She sang 'I Will Always Love You'. I noticed she was looking at Michael all the time. It was beautiful, and everyone was clapping. She then said, "We have another surprise for you. Please welcome Natalie, my sister, on stage to sing with me." They sang 'I Have Nothing'. The crowd went mad. Natalie came and sat down and left Bene to go through another six songs.

Chloe said, "You kept that voice a secret. You are very good. So is Bene. You should both be on stage." Stan agreed. Michael did not take his eyes off Bene all the time she was on stage.

When she came back, Michael met her and said, "That was awesome," and kissed her in front of everyone. Bene was embarrassed, but smiled and sat back down. "Sorry, Bene," he said. "Did I go too far?"

"Oh, no, it just surprised me."

People kept coming to our table and chatting to Bene and Natalie. They were all wondering when they were going to be there again so they could bring more friends.

"See how good you are for my business?"

"Don't you mean our business?"

"Of course," I said, and kissed her.

The MC said, "Last song of the evening. Please welcome Natalie to the stage to sing her beautiful rendition of the Roberta Flack classic 'The First Time Ever I Saw Your Face'." The crowd was already clapping so she had to sing it now.

Natalie was absolutely wonderful. The crowd was all still there. The place was packed. It was midnight – everyone was on their feet.

Bene said, "I must learn that one." Michael grabbed Bene's hand and led her outside. We all followed ten minutes later, and they were still kissing around the corner.

"Come on, you two, time to go home."

"One more kiss," she said.

"OK, five minutes," we said.

Chapter 3

It was the Friday before the wedding. Stan was getting worried. Tommaso had not been found. He could still be very dangerous. He would have revenge on his mind.

Chloe had said she was selling her house and asked if she could move in permanently. She said she loved me. I definitely love her. She did say no marriage plans for a while though. I agreed. We had both been down that road before.

Bene and Michael had been out together every night now. He had stayed the last two nights and they were looking happy. She stayed in one night and sat down and said she would like to talk. She said that her and Michael had found each other again and asked if he could come with us on honeymoon as well. We had seen this coming as they were sleeping together again. Natalie cuddled her and said, "Is that what you want or what Michael wants?"

She paused. "I think that is what I want, but I keep thinking about what happened before."

"What about your career in singing?"

"I want to record here in England. I need some really good songs of my own."

"Yes, we can help you with that. We sent some of your songs to producers and they have writers that can help you." Natalie said, "Do you trust me? I have some ideas and we could work on them together, but come on your own with us. Do you love him?"

"Definitely," she said.

"Does he love you?"

"He says he does."

"You are not sure you fully trust him yet."

"Is it that obvious?" she said.

Natalie said, "Invite him over tonight. He is not expecting it, and we will all have a chat."

She rang his number and a woman answered. Bene started crying. Natalie grabbed the phone and said, "Who is this?"

"I am Angela, Michael's sister. Is Michael there?"

"Yes, he is in the shower. I will call him for you. Bene, it is his sister."

She did not know he had a sister – he had never mentioned it.

"Hello, Michael, Natalie here, can you come over please for a chat? OK, will be there in fifteen minutes."

Bene was still recovering from the shock. "I have been in his house and had never seen any signs of a sister."

Michael knocked on the door. "I brought my sister with me. She thought you seemed worried." They walked in.

"Angela Jones," Bene gasped. She was about ten years older than Michael. "You used to sing with the 'Mind Bangers'. Yes, you married Terry Jones, the lead guitarist."

She said, "Yes, I have just come back off tour. I was so pleased when he told me you had got back together. He had been such a misery since you broke up."

"Sorry, Angela, I did not know Michael had a sister."

"OK, what did you want to see me about?"

"It is about going away with Natalie and Alan. You don't want me there, do you?" Michael said.

Angela said, "Michael, stop it. You are lucky that Bene is going out with you at all after the way you treated her."

"Sorry, yes," he said, "but I am afraid you will not come back to me."

"Don't be silly. We have so much ahead of us. I am going to be based here to launch my singing career. I want to share it with you. Come here you fool," and she cuddled him. "Natalie and I want to spend time as well as write songs together."

Angela said, "Come home now, Michael. These people have plans to do." They left quite happy. "You will see her tomorrow at the wedding."

Chapter 4

The big day had arrived. Natalie and Bene took my car around to Stan and Chloe's to get ready. Steve turned up; he was my best man. The only long-term friend I had.

Although it was a Registry Office, it was quite large and was filling up. Steve and I waited for the girls to turn up.

Natalie arrived and was walking towards me; I was welling up with happiness. She was a beautiful bride; her dress was a very expensive white wedding gown; she was followed by two beautiful bridesmaids in equally expensive blue gowns. I noticed that Stan was standing guard at the door with two plain clothes. The wedding went perfectly, and Miss Natalie James became Mrs Natalie Ford.

After the ceremony, we headed back to our restaurant venue. We all found our seats and waited for the meal to begin. It was Italian, of course.

After a splendid meal, the toasts began. Chloe unexpectedly stood up and made such an impressive speech about her special friend Natalie. Natalie was in tears. She jumped up and gave Chloe a big hug.

I stood up in the end and gave a special announcement about Natalie and my wealth. How we were both shareholders in the company. I made Steve stand up and said, "Steve is now the main shareholder and CEO of the company." Natalie and I were going to start taking a more backseat role from now on.

"There are two major promotions." There was a drum roll.

"Caroline will be taking over as permanent head of the Chelmsford branch with more expansion in the future for the office. Finally, this has been the most guarded secret. Chloe, please stand up. Please meet our new personal secretary."

Now Chloe was crying. "Thank you so much," she sobbed, "I will not let you down." This time Chloe got up and came and hugged us both. "How about that, receptionist to personal secretary in six months."

Bene then got up and said, "Natalie and Alan to the dance floor for the first dance." She rushed to the microphone and sang, guess what? 'I Will Always Love You'.

When she finished, I kissed Natalie and said, "I will always love you."

She said, "I will always love you as well."

I thought, *this is the happiest time of my life. Dancing with my beautiful bride.*

The time came for Natalie and I to leave; we were going back to the flat to change and head off to a secret location for the night. Not even Steve or Bene knew. Natalie whispered in Bene's ear, "The flat is yours tonight, but be ready to leave at eleven a.m. tomorrow.

They hugged and Bene said, "Thank you, sister. I love you so much."

Natalie

Michael

Chapter 1

Natalie and I arrived back at the flat from our first night as Mr and Mrs Ford. Bene was there with her cases all packed and ready. We had to rush as we were a bit late. We had hired a Limo to take us to the airport. Fortunately, everything was ready to pack, and we were soon on the way to the airport.

Bene seemed really happy. "I have something to tell you," she said. "Michael asked me to marry him."

Natalie said, "What did you say?"

"I did not say no, but ask me again when we get back."

Natalie cuddled her and said, "I am so happy for you."

Bene said, "I am going to say yes when we get back. He has shown me how much he loves me."

"Are you sure, Bene? It has been so quick."

"It just feels right," she said. "I do love him so much, I always did. I trust him this time."

Michael left the flat early; he was not disappointed that Bene had not said yes to his proposal, but she had said to ask her again when they got back. She is going to say yes, because she did not say no. *He was so excited that he woke Angela up when he got home to tell her. She said, "Don't mess it up this time."*

"I won't," Michael said. "I have never been so sure of anything in my life. I love her. She is the most beautiful girl in the world."

Chapter 2

Chloe went in to work on the Monday. A new girl, Michele, was sitting at what was her desk. "Good morning, Chloe," she said brightly. "Please let me show you to your new office." This all felt so weird. She had been given Natalie's office. Her name, Chloe Wells, was on the door with the job title, 'Personal Assistant'. She went in and sat in the lush chair.

She said, "Thank you, Michele. We must have a chat later." Michele smiled and said she would like that.

There were two letters on her desk. One was from Natalie, and one was an official-looking brown envelope. She opened the official one first. It was her new contract of employment. It described in detail what her role would entail. She was thinking, I can do this. She got to the end where it said annual salary and screamed with delight. Caroline rushed in from her office next door.

"Chloe, what is wrong?"

Chloe said, "Nothing, but I have just read my contract and look at this."

Annual salary £100,000 with incremental annual increase. Caroline smiled and said, "You have earned it. You may not have known it, but Natalie had been giving you tasks way above your job description. Everyone noticed how competent you had become. Natalie can't afford to lose you. Come into my office. I will show you something."

It was Caroline's new contract. "Look at the bottom," she said. Annual salary, £120,000. I have been given the added responsibility of implementing the new Action Plan across the whole company. I am virtually Steve's deputy." They hugged and congratulated each other.

Chloe went back to her new office and opened Natalie's letter.

Dear Chloe,

You have been my best friend here and have proved to me what you are capable of. I have been testing you for months and you proved to me that you are very competent. It has been, if you like, a three-month long interview. You passed with flying colours, and have now been rewarded. Please remain my best friend and sign the contract.

Love you loads,
Natalie

Chloe had tears in her eyes. She rang Stan and told him the good news. He said, "Let us celebrate tonight, then. Where do you want to go?"

"Alan's Italian," she said. "It is on me as well. My new salary is £100,000 per year." Stan had to sit down. He said that was more than twice what he earned a year.

Chloe had a walk around the offices and had a chat with everyone. Michael was trying to attract her attention. She went over and he whispered, "I have asked Bene to marry me."

"What did she say?"

"She said, ask me again when we get back."

Chloe said, "She is going to say yes, you know."

He said, "I hope so. I love her so much. I want your advice."

Chloe said, "Come to my office in five minutes and bring two cups of coffee."

He gave a big grin and said, "Yes, Ma'am."

He came to Chloe's office and said what he had in mind.

Chloe said, "You do not need my help, you have it all worked out."

He said thank you and left with a big grin on his face. Chloe thought that if that young man did that for her, she would marry him in an instant. Chloe's phone started ringing continuously. The millionaire's fairy tale romance had got out, and all the local press wanted an interview. Even a national tabloid had got hold of the story. Now she would have to earn her new salary.

Stan took Chloe to the restaurant. He looked a bit on edge. Chloe asked, "What is wrong?" looking very concerned.

The waiter arrived with champagne. "Compliments of the owner," he said. The waiter left.

Stan said, "I am so sorry, but I can't do this anymore."

Tears were welling Chloe's eyes.

"I need more stability in my life."

"What do you mean?"

"I have been thinking, and have changed my mind. Forgive me," he said.

Chloe was crying now. "Don't you love me anymore?"

Stan got down on one knee and said, "Chloe, I can't live without you anymore. Will you marry me?" He fished out a diamond ring.

Chloe said, "You big fool softie, of course I will. I just did not want to pressurise you. You arranged the champagne, didn't you?" He nodded, and she kissed him. "I know you are only after my money really."

They laughed together all evening. Chloe thought, My life is nearly complete now.

Chapter 3

The honeymoon was passing in a blur. We had only left the island twice for a quick trip to Rome and another to Venice. The girls had hardly left the beach and were humming, singing and writing songs. They had written ten so far. Bene sat at her electric organ a few times to sing them to me. By the Saturday before we were due to leave, we all had amazing suntans. The girls had even gone topless around the pool at the mansion.

On the Saturday evening, Stan rang. He said, "Can you talk?"

"Just a minute." The girls were chatting to Sofia, so I walked into the garden. "What is wrong?"

"Very bad news, I am afraid. Michael has been shot. He is in hospital, but they think he may not survive. Do you want me to tell Bene?" I said that I would do it.

"Do what?" The girls had crept out behind me.

"That was Stan."

"What has happened?"

"Come back inside and sit down." I looked at Bene and said, "I am so sorry, but Michael has been shot."

Bene was crying now. "Is he OK?"

"He is in a very critical condition in hospital. They don't think he is going to survive."

Bene was totally distraught. "I was going to tell him 'yes' when we got back."

Bene got up and ran to her room, crying profusely. Natalie

followed her. Sofia was crying as well. "Bene was telling me about Michael, and how she was in love. I did not know she was thinking of marrying him. If you listened to a couple of the songs she wrote. You would know she was going to say yes."

An hour later, Natalie and Bene re-appeared. They both were very red-eyed. Bene asked, "What happened?"

"It appears he was in the flat setting up a surprise for you. He had finished and was on his way out when someone attacked him. We believe that they were after us. He was shot three times. The neighbours reported gunshots and the police arrived quickly, Stan was there in minutes. The ambulance arrived ten minutes later. They were doing CPR all the way to the hospital, but he was losing a lot of blood."

"What was he doing?" I showed her the pictures. On the door there was a heart with an arrow with words 'Benedetta and Michael'. In the room, in rose petals, was written 'I love you Bene, will you please marry me?'

That did it; Bene and Natalie were both crying again. Bene shouted, "YES, YES, YES."

Just then, Lorenzo walked in and saw all the red eyes. "What has happened?" he said.

Bene got up and rushed to her father's arms. "Daddy, Michael has been shot. They do not think he will survive."

"Where is he?"

I said, "Broomfield hospital, Chelmsford, England."

Lorenzo quickly took charge. "Right, you three get packed. Hand luggage only. I will get the private jet to fly you all the way."

Bene said, "Thank you, Daddy. I love you."

He picked up the phone and said, "Get ready, then."

It was good it got the girls moving. I said, "Pack mine for

me, I need to make some calls."

Lorenzo called the airport and the flight crew and told them why. The plane would be ready in forty-five minutes. "The only hold could be the flight plan. You have not eaten, so I will arrange a meal on board. I know a trauma specialist. He is supposed to be the best in the world. He is American, but is in Paris at the moment. Money is no object here; my daughter's happiness is at stake."

I rang Chloe; she said she would arrange everything her end. She sobbed, "I know what Michael had done for Bene. This is so sad. How is Bene?"

"Not good," I said. "We are all upset. Congratulations, by the way."

"Thank you, but it does not seem so good now. Send our love and will see you soon."

"Hang on. Lorenzo will be contacting you with other arrangements."

"OK," she said, "and so sorry again."

Natalie came down first. I said, "Where is Bene?"

"Still packing in her room, she was talking to Sofia."

"OK, but she needs to hurry." Natalie took our two small cases to the door and went back up to get Bene.

Chapter 4

When the plane had taken off, we made sure that Bene was between us. We kept asking her questions about Michael. Most it we already knew, but we needed to keep her talking. I was thinking that this wonderful young lady had done nothing to deserve this. When we landed, it was a quick dash through customs and into the waiting limo. We went straight to the hospital. Michael's sister was there. Dr Bolton had arrived from Paris before us and was examining Michael. Michael's parents came rushing in. It was the first time we had met the Davenports. Bene had met them a couple of times two years ago. "The specialist is in with him at the moment." Just then, Dr Bolton came out and took us all into an office as he did not want to repeat what he had to say.

Dr Bolton cleared his throat and said we had two choices. One, do nothing, with a 5% chance of survival, or two, operate, after which he may not survive. He estimated a 30% survival rate if he got through the operation. John Davenport asked, "If he survives the operation, will he be able to live a normal life?"

The doctor said, "Yes, after about six months."

Bene looked pleadingly at him and said, "Please let them operate. I love him so much."

John said, "It looks like that is the best option." Bene went up and hugged them both.

"We will get the theatre ready and will operate as soon as possible," said Dr Bolton, and he dashed off. The staff nurse then came in with consent forms to sign. The operation was going to take most of the night even with the team of three surgeons.

I asked Bene if she wanted to go home or if we should all book a hotel room.

"I definitely want to go home and lay in the bed. Michael has done so much, and it will feel like I am laying with him."

Stan rang and said, "we have him. Tommaso had been trying to leave from Dover on the ferry. He has been arrested and is being interviewed by us and Interpol. Will keep you in touch."

It was a very long night, and Michael survived the operation. Now we just had to wait. The longer Michael survived, the better his chances.

Bene poured herself into her singing. We went with her every day. She had a single to release, and the album was nearly finished after a month. Bene had now learned to pour all her emotion into a song. A tragedy had done that for her.

Michael woke from his coma after a month, and the first thing he saw was Bene looking at him. He said, "hello, beautiful." Bene cried with joy this time.

Chapter 5

Bene visited Michael in hospital every day, and after six months he walked out on his own. As soon as he was out of the door, he went on one knee and said, "Benedetta Romano. Will you be my wife and marry me?" Bene said yes without hesitation.

He put a ring on her finger. She so deserved to be happy again. Her single 'Be Mine Forever' made it to the number one spot on the UK charts. The album was still in the top ten after three months. She has been on many talk shows now, and her story also helped escalate her up the charts. There were two collaborations on the album. Both with Natalie. As soon as Michael is able, they are going to tour Europe and the US. Chloe is still wearing her engagement ring. They have both been so busy, but are still so much in love. They have booked the wedding for next year.

Natalie is seven months pregnant, and is getting quite large. It suits her. She looks more radiant than ever. The latest scan showed we are having twin girls.